THE
WINTER
WOLF

www.hollywebbanimalstories.com

STRIPES PUBLISHING
An imprint of Little Tiger Press
1 The Coda Centre, 189 Munster Road,
London SW6 6AW

This paperback edition first published
in Great Britain in 2016.

ISBN: 978-1-84715-541-2

A CIP catalogue record for this book is available
from the British Library.

Printed and bound in the UK.

2 4 6 8 10 9 7 5 3

THE
WINTER
WOLF

HOLLY WEBB

Stripes

For Robin and William

~ HOLLY WEBB

For Dan

~ JO

12th October, 1873

The creek is frozen near solid now. Pa says this is the hardest winter he has ever seen. There was frost on the inside of the windows and the cabin walls this morning when we got up, even though Ma kept the stove burning low through the night. I woke up in the middle of the night shivering, with the wind howling all around us. It felt like hours before I got back to sleep, and all that time I kept thinking that the wind was a wolf padding round the cabin, looking for a way in. The drifts are up to the eaves, and Pa and I dig our way out each morning to get to the stable and feed the horses and the cow.

This morning, I noticed huge icicles hanging from the edges of the cabin roof where the sun melted the snow, and then it's dripped and frozen again overnight. Seeing them sparkle made me think of Grace. Last year, Pa let me knock two of them down with his hammer, and Grace and me used them for a swordfight, up and down the big room, till mine broke in three pieces and Pa said Grace was the winner. I wish I hadn't sulked about it now. She was so pleased to have won.

CHAPTER
ONE

Tangled branches tapped at the windows as the car nosed down the track towards the house. Amelia shivered happily. It was a bit like a fairy tale, this huge, old, abandoned house, deep in the countryside. There had been a sign at the end of the track, half grown over with ivy. Amelia had just about been able to see that it said "Allan House". It felt like a proper adventure, travelling late into the night, all the way up to Scotland. They hadn't passed another car for ages, winding along those tiny lanes in the dark.

But as they climbed out of the car, stretching and then shuffling wearily towards the door, Amelia pressed close against her big sister, Bella. She was shy with strangers, and she could hardly remember her cousins at all. Anya was the same age as Bella, Mum had said. Lara was another year older. Tom was ten, a few months older than Amelia. Bella said she remembered Anya and Lara perfectly, and she was looking forward to seeing them again. Amelia had a horrible feeling that the older girls weren't going to want her hanging around. She was going to be stuck with this boy, Tom. Just because they were cousins, it didn't mean she was going to get on with him. It was strange, spending Christmas all together, in a house that none of them knew.

Amelia blinked in the sudden golden glow as the front door opened, and then there were loud, excited voices all around, and people laughing and hugging and pulling them inside. Amelia shrank against the wall, watching as her mum kissed a tiny, dark-haired woman who looked amazingly like Mum did. That must be Mum's cousin Laura, Amelia realized. She hadn't expected them to look so similar. And the two girls with their arms round Bella were their second cousins.

"And this must be Amelia!" Laura swung round to hug her now, and twirled her fingers in Amelia's dark curls.

Amelia tried to smile – people always did that, and she had to pretend she didn't mind.

"Sorry, Amelia, I couldn't resist – they're so pretty," Laura told her, smiling. Laura was her first cousin once removed. Something like that, anyway. But Amelia could hardly call her that. Mum had said it would be simplest just to call her Aunt Laura.

"Hi," Amelia whispered.

"Do you remember Tom at all?" Aunt Laura asked, ushering a reluctant-looking boy towards Amelia. "You haven't seen each other for, oh, about three years, so you probably don't…"

Amelia saw that the boy had dark, floppy hair, and that he was taller than she was (almost everyone was – she was used to it by now). Then she spotted the huge tawny and silver dog that was standing behind him. She took a step back, pressing her hands flat against the faded wallpaper, wishing it would open up behind her so she could get away. Mum had told her that their cousins had a dog and Amelia had been worrying about it for weeks. She'd even woken up in the night panicking a couple of times. But even then, in the dark, she hadn't imagined a dog *that* big…

"Oh, so this is your dog," her mum said, smiling a little worriedly. "Amelia has a bit of a thing about dogs. Is it a he?" she added, looking at the dog uncertainly.

Amelia had no idea how anyone would tell if the dog was a boy or a girl. All she could see were its quivering ears, lots of shaggy brownish-grey fur and its teeth… It looked like some sort of wolf. And it was quite possibly the biggest dog she had ever seen. Even bigger than that horrible dog in the park that had knocked her over a couple of years ago. The owner had tried to tell her that the dog was just excited, but it had barked and barked, right in her face, and Amelia had never felt so scared.

"I'm sure he's friendly, Amelia," her mum said gently, reaching out a hand to her, but the dog was in between them, and Amelia couldn't bring herself to step past it.

She edged further away, and then

stopped, realizing that she was right up against the front door. She couldn't go any further, and now the dog was padding towards her, sniffing at her with interest.

"Hey!" Bella turned round from talking to the other girls, and stepped in front of the dog. "Yes, you're lovely, aren't you? But you have to leave Amelia alone, she's not a dog person." She held out her hand for the dog to sniff, and it licked her. Bella laughed, but just the sight of that great red tongue made Amelia shudder.

"Are you really frightened of dogs?" Tom asked, staring at her disgustedly.

"A dog knocked Amelia over in the park," Mum explained, coming to put her arm round Amelia's shoulders. "It was a big dog, and she got a shock."

"But Freddie's not fierce," Tom objected. "He even lets the little girl next door ride on his back." Freddie swooshed his massive tail as he heard his name, and Amelia pressed herself against her mum. She knew it was stupid to be scared – she could see that Freddie was friendly – but telling herself that didn't help. Her heart was thumping so hard she was sure everyone else could hear it, too.

"Take Freddie and put him in the kitchen, Tom," Aunt Laura said firmly, and Tom marched off, muttering crossly, with Freddie lumbering along behind.

"Are you all right?" Bella nudged Amelia.

"Yes," Amelia whispered. But she wasn't. They were staying here for a whole week. It was Christmas in three days.

They were going to gather round the tree to sing carols and make a gingerbread house, and do all of Amelia's favourite Christmas things. It was meant to be the most special time of the year, and now it was ruined. She was going to spend the whole of Christmas hiding from a dog.

Amelia sat on the wide windowsill in her bedroom, wrapped in a woollen blanket she'd found at the bottom of the wardrobe. It was brown and hairy and it had holes in, but it was very warm against the freezing wind that was whistling round the house and doing its best to get inside. Amelia was wearing her fingerless gloves as she wrote in her diary. It had been a Christmas present from her gran last year, and she managed to write in it most days, even if it was only things like, *Hate Mrs Turner*, and *Wish homework had never been invented.* But now they were at Allan House, there seemed to be a lot to write about – or at least, there was more time to write. If she went downstairs and tried to watch TV, Tom always seemed to turn up with Freddie. It was as if he was following her. And Bella kept nicking the tablet they were supposed to share.

It still isn't snowing, Amelia wrote, peering sadly out of the window. The view was very beautiful, in a grey sort of way. The hills rose up behind the house in great, fat sweeps, covered in green turf that looked like velvet, though it wasn't at all velvety when you got close up, because Amelia had checked.

When Mum had told them excitedly about the house, and how it belonged to her and Aunt Laura now, and they were going to stay in it for Christmas, she had practically promised it would snow. *Sledging*, she had said enthusiastically. *Snowmen. Snowball fights!*

Actually, Amelia thought, resting her cheek against the cold glass for a moment, that was the one good thing about no snow. She was pretty sure that Tom would be lethal with a snowball. And he'd probably cheat and just stuff snow down the back of her neck as well. She shivered, and slid down from the windowsill, wrapping the blanket tighter like a cloak. She would go and explore, she decided. Allan House was huge, and even though this was the second whole day they'd been here, Amelia was pretty sure she hadn't seen all of it. The house seemed to have a lot more corners than any house she'd been in before. Every time she thought she'd got to the end of it, there would be another little passageway.

She opened her bedroom door and peered round it cautiously. But no paws were padding along the wooden floorboards anywhere close. Letting out a relieved breath, Amelia sneaked into the passageway and looked thoughtfully from side to side. She would head away from the stairs, she decided. Further along, the passage stretched into shadows beyond a huge old wooden cupboard, and it looked exciting. She set off to explore, with the hairy blanket trailing the floor behind her, sweeping up dust.

Until a few months ago, the house had belonged to one of Mum and Laura's aunts, but Amelia had never met her. She couldn't imagine the old lady – she had been very old, Mum said – living here all on her own. Surely she had been lonely in such a big house far away from any neighbours? But perhaps that was why it was so full of things. Ornaments and candlesticks and rugs and all those pictures.

Amelia stopped to look at the painting

just opposite Bella's room. It was dark in the passageway, as there were wooden shutters closed over the window, but even in the dimness, the colours glowed. A fire blazed in the middle of the canvas, casting an eerie light on the man sitting behind it. He was wrapped in a dark, hairy blanket, just like Amelia's. Behind him, another man was sleeping in a sort of hut, made of old branches piled together. Perhaps they were hunters, Amelia thought. It looked like they were deep in a wood. She leaned closer, drawn in by the glowing flames. The sparks were flying up from the fire and glittering in the darkness, and the firelight spread a charmed circle round the two men. But beyond it the trees were thick and dark, and she was sure that there were creatures waiting just on the edge of the light.

Amelia shivered. Probably wolves, even bigger and scarier than Freddie. She stepped back, and saw a name written in the bottom corner of the painting. She squinted down at the signature, trying to make it out, and then smiled delightedly. Noah Allan. The man the house was named after! Mum had told them about him – that he had been born in America, but he'd travelled to France to study. Then he had visited friends in Scotland, and found the dramatic landscape so perfect to paint that he'd settled here. He was Amelia's great-great-great-grandfather – except that she couldn't remember quite how many greats there should be. But she knew he had been born more than a hundred and fifty years ago. Her mum had told her that there was a very famous Noah Allan painting in a gallery in London, of a girl and a wolf. They'd go and see it one day, Mum had said.

Amelia was so excited to find another painting by their ancestor that it took her a moment to hear the scuffling and tapping of claws. She clutched the blanket round her in a panic. Tom and that enormous dog were coming up the stairs!

Amelia scuttled down the passageway. She'd done her best to avoid being alone with Tom. He obviously thought she was stupid because she was frightened of dogs and he moaned about having to shut Freddie up during meals, in case he scared Amelia. But Anya had told Amelia that it made it much easier to eat breakfast – if Freddie was around he could have a piece of toast out of your hand in three seconds flat.

Freddie was snuffling his way along the passage now, and Amelia cursed herself for being stupid – why hadn't she just nipped back into her own bedroom? They would catch up with her any moment, and Freddie would sniff at her, and Tom wouldn't make him stop, Amelia knew he wouldn't. He'd just laugh.

Amelia ducked round the huge wooden cupboard, and stood there in the shadows, hoping they'd go straight past. But she could hear Freddie sniffing at everything, and Tom sniggering as the dust made the huge dog sneeze. There was no way Freddie was going to miss her. And it would be obvious that she was hiding, and Tom would tell everyone, like it was a great big joke.

Amelia leaned back, trying to wriggle into the corner where the cupboard wasn't pushed right up against the wall. Except that her blanket was catching on something sticking out of the wall. She looked round cautiously and realized that she wasn't leaning on a wall at all.

It was a door.

15th October, 1873

Mr Wright and Joshua came by this morning. I haven't seen Joshua since they helped with killing the pig a few weeks back, and I haven't missed him. Sometimes I wish we had neighbours closer by, but then they might be like him. I swear he spent the whole visit smirking at me and pulling faces.

They came to tell us that they'd seen a wolf slinking round their cabin. That had Pa listening. He doesn't always pay attention to Mr Wright - says he's always complaining about something, and he borrows tools and brings them back dirty. But the Wrights are the only other family between here and the town, and that's a day's journey. So it's best to keep friends with them, even if it means listening to Samson Wright moan, Pa says.

Mr Wright said their dogs had been acting funny for a couple of nights, and he thought there was something around. He guessed it was a bear – there's a big old black bear that Pa saw a few times earlier in the autumn, sniffing round the pigpen. But then in the morning he found tracks in the snow and he knew it was a wolf. Just one, Mr Wright said, and I could see Pa looking funny at that, as though he thought it was odd to have only one wolf, when they almost always hunt in packs. I suppose that means it's a loner, and that means trouble. A lone wolf is desperate. I wonder if it really was a wolf I heard, then, a few nights back?

Mr Wright and Joshua sat up watching for it last night, and Joshua got a shot at the wolf, but only just clipped it, he reckons. It ran off, anyways. He's acting like he's some mighty hero, shooting a wolf, but if all he's done is wound the poor beast, now it's going to be even more maddened and fierce.

Pa's sitting up late tonight, making bullets.

CHAPTER
TWO

A melia slid up the latch – that was what the blanket had got caught on, she realized. She eased the door open, holding her breath and waiting for it to creak. But it didn't. A faint bar of light shone out into the passage, and Amelia wormed her way round the door. It opened just wide enough to let her through. There was no rush of feet or scurry of paws as she drew the door shut again behind her. Tom and Freddie hadn't heard.

In front of her was a steep, narrow staircase, thick with dust. Amelia glanced back at the door, and tested the first step with her foot to see if it creaked. The step gave a faint sigh, and Amelia thought it almost sounded pleased, but it was only the old wood giving under her weight. She tiptoed up the rest of the little staircase, trying hard not to sneeze with all the dust. Below her she could hear Tom talking to Freddie, but he seemed very far away. She was somehow certain that he didn't know about the door. This place belonged to her.

The stairs opened up into a tiny, light-filled room. This must be the very top of the house, Amelia decided, where those two little windows were, right up in the roof. High up here, there was even a pale glow of sunlight, shimmering through the dirty glass.

The attic was full of boxes – not the boring cardboard sort that were stacked up in the loft at home, full of Amelia's outgrown baby clothes and old wellingtons. Here there were wooden packing crates, fat trunks and old leather suitcases, plastered with faded labels. Ancient pieces of furniture were clustered around as well: an armchair with half its stuffing escaping, and a spindly little table, piled high with books. Amelia wrapped the blanket tighter round her shoulders – it was even colder up here, right under the roof.

Curiously, she turned over the books on the little table and found that they were school books – the one on top had a faded brown cover, and was full of odd little stories in French. At least, Amelia thought it was French. There was a picture of a very cross little girl on the first page, with an even crosser cat in her arms.

Amelia crouched down in front of a big leather trunk and pushed hopefully at the brass clasp holding it shut. It was stiff, but then it sprang open, making her jump. She held her breath as she lifted up the lid, wondering who had been the last person to look inside. Maybe no one had opened the trunk since it had been hauled up here. She sniffed cautiously as she leaned the lid against the armchair, but the clothes in the trunk smelled faintly of herbs and weren't at all musty or damp. Carefully, Amelia lifted out the dark garments, unfolding them and holding them up. Two jackets, a heavy, checked woollen coat, several patched and faded shirts, and a hat that made Amelia shudder. She was sure that the soft, dark fur of the hat was real. But she supposed that a long time ago, a fur hat would have been the best way to keep warm. She didn't want to try it on, though.

The jackets and shirts were big, about Amelia's father's size, she thought, but the coat looked smaller, as though it had been made for a child. Amelia stroked the wooden buttons, satin smooth, and wondered who had carved them. Then, all of a sudden, she slid the blanket off her shoulders, and pulled on the coat instead, buttoning it down the front, and turning the wide collar up round her ears to keep herself warm. She picked her way across the floor to an old mirror that leaned against another of the wooden chests, then turned and swayed in front of it, trying to catch a glimpse of herself in the mottled glass. The coat was shapeless, and faded, but very warm. Its lining was quilted, and Amelia felt as though she was wearing a duvet. She peered into the mirror one last time, and sank her hands into the deep pockets. Her fingers were stiffening up from the cold.

The right-hand pocket was empty, but in the left-hand one, Amelia's fingers closed round a small, flat packet. She pulled it out and walked over to the armchair under the window to get a better look at what she'd found.

A notebook? No – Amelia prised open the stiff old pages, and saw the scrawled handwriting and the date written at the top of the page.

16th October, 1873.

A diary.

Amelia swallowed, and her hands shook with excitement. It was more than a hundred and forty years old! She'd seen ancient things before in museums, even Egyptian mummies from thousands of years ago. But somehow holding this little book in her own hands felt very different. It might even have belonged to one of her relatives, since this house was her family's. The spidery brown writing felt like a message from the past:

Bitter cold again today. Wind howling around the cabin so loud you'd swear it was alive and trying to get in. Pa says we need to plaster mud over the chinks in the walls again come springtime.

Amelia shivered. That was just what she had felt, earlier on in her room. But at least she was in a house, a big stone-built house that had been here for hundreds of years. A cabin didn't sound very warm at all, especially if it had holes in the walls.

The writing was so faded that it was hard to read in places. She was frowning over it, trying to puzzle out the rest of the entry, when she heard voices calling from below – impatient voices that sounded as if they might have been shouting for a while.

"Amelia! Amelia, are you asleep up there? Come on, we're all going for a walk."

Amelia jumped up, wriggling out of the heavy coat, before draping it over the chair. She looked for a second at the diary, but for some reason she didn't want to take it with her. It belonged up here, with the old trunk. And it was a secret – *her* secret.

"I'll come back," she whispered, as she started down the wooden stairs. It was

silly, talking to a book, but she didn't care.
And she *would* come back, just as soon as
she could slip away.

17th October, 1873

Pa hasn't seen any sign of the wolf. He's beginning to think that Mr Wright is seeing things, I reckon. There haven't been any tracks round our cabin, so I've been out setting snares as usual. I can't deny that I've been looking over my shoulder a lot, though. The wind blowing through the trees can sound a lot like a wolf when you know there's one about. At least it's not a puma! Wolves can't climb trees, and I don't like the thought of a great big cat stretched out on a branch, just waiting for me to walk by underneath!

18th October, 1873

Well, Mr Wright and Joshua weren't imagining it, after all. I've seen the wolf. Ma sent me to fetch water from the spring, and I was on my way back with the bucket when I saw it. Just standing there, looking at me! I wanted to scream and run, but Pa's always said that wolves are like dogs. They like to chase, and if you run, they'll run after you, except they go lickety-split. So I just stood there and stared back at him.

That's when I realized - it was a pup. I've seen wolves, full-grown ones, and they're bigger than our dogs, even if they can be skinny sometimes. They're big at the shoulders, and the old dog wolves have great ruffs of fur round their necks. This wolf watching me was just a pup. And he was more scared than I was, I reckoned, after we'd stood there staring at each other for a full minute.

The more I looked at him, the more I thought he couldn't be the wolf that Joshua took a shot at. He's only a pup and he's not been hurt at all – Joshua said he saw blood. He didn't look fierce, either. He was like a big gangly puppy – all paws.

Slowly, I crouched down, waiting and watching in case he decided to spring. But he didn't – he just looked, shuffling his fat paws in the snow like he was nervous. So I clapped my mittens on my knees and called to him, like he was one of the dogs. I know I should have gone home straight

away and called Pa and told him to get his
gun, but I couldn't.

Maybe Pa wouldn't have shot him, anyway.
He never hunts deer in the springtime, when
the does are looking after their young. So
he wouldn't shoot a wolf pup, would he?

Except, he'd probably say that the pup
would grow up to be a danger. He'd be right,
too. A young wolf like that can't know how
to hunt properly yet, and if it's all on its
own, there's no one to teach it. So all it
can do is go after people, and our livestock,
the horses and the cow. If Grace was still
with us, it wouldn't be long before that wolf
could eat her up, even if it is only a pup.

So I shouldn't have done what I did.

But he came to me. As friendly as our
dogs, Sammy and Ned. He let me rub his ears
and he sniffed at my coat, which probably

smelled of rabbits. And then he licked my face. When I went to walk away – Ma was still waiting for that water – he followed me.

Well, I stopped then, of course. I couldn't take a wolf pup back home, no matter how friendly he was. But I had to do something about him. Was he lost? I couldn't work it out. He shouldn't have been on his own, a pup like that.

I crouched there, petting his ears, and that was when I worked it out. He wasn't the wolf Joshua shot – that was his mother. It makes sense, I'm sure of it. She came hunting, and Joshua wounded her, so now she's run off, or she's hiding out somewhere till she's better. Or she died, I suppose, but Joshua's the worst shot I've ever seen, so I reckon not. Meanwhile, her pup's come looking for her. We're not that far away from the Wrights' place. He's tried to track his mother and got himself lost and found me instead.

So now I've got myself a wolf pup.

CHAPTER
THREE

A melia woke up, breathing fast in the darkness. She had been dreaming about that dog again, the one in the park, and it had left her so scared that she was shaking.

She peered out at her room, but she couldn't see anything at all. At home, even in the darkest part of the night, there was a dull orange glow from the streetlamp outside her window. Here there were no lights at all, and the darkness was so thick Amelia felt like she could touch it.

She fished around on the bedside table for her torch and flicked it on. The glowing amber beam danced over the walls, and Amelia caught her breath at last. Freddie was downstairs, shut in. It had only been a dream. But she didn't want to go back to sleep, in case she dreamed it all over again. She shone the torch over the floor, wondering where her book had got to – under the bed, maybe? She wished she hadn't left the diary upstairs. She wanted to know more about the person writing it, and the snowy winter, and the wolf pup.

Her torch beam flickered upwards over the window, and Amelia gave a little excited gasp, sitting up straight in bed and forgetting about the dark, and the dog.

It was snowing! At last! She scrambled out of bed, pulling the duvet with her, and went over to kneel up on the window seat and look.

The flakes were swirling down thickly, but it was hard to see if it was settling or not, with the torch reflecting off the black glass. She undid the window catch to peer out for a moment and sighed delightedly. Already the trees outside the window had a thin, crisp coating of white, like icing sugar. And the sky was heavy with fat, yellowish-tinged snow clouds. It looked as though the snow could go on falling for a while. She huddled the duvet closer around her and stared at the whirling whiteness.

Real, proper snow. Maybe Christmas would be a little bit Christmassy after all.

"Don't you want to come out on the sledge?" Bella asked coaxingly, putting her arm round Amelia. Bella had her big fluffy jacket on, and a sweater and a hoodie underneath, and her cheeks were pink. They'd hardly finished breakfast, and already everyone was out in the snow. Tom had been out in it as soon as it got light.

Amelia shook her head. Through the window she could see Tom and Freddie racing around outside. Tom was throwing snowballs, and Freddie was chasing after them. It was quite funny, really – Freddie kept trying to pick up the collapsed snowballs in his mouth. The mush of snow got all over his long nose and every time he'd shake his head and give Tom a confused sort of look.

But even when he was confused and funny, Freddie was still huge. And his teeth were almost as white as the snowballs. Amelia didn't want him chasing her.

"No. It's too cold. And my nose is all blocked up – I don't want to make it worse," she told Bella. She was pretty sure Bella didn't believe her, but her big sister just sighed, and went out to join Anya and Lara, who were pulling the sledge up the hill.

Amelia watched them for a few minutes, and then she padded quietly along the hallway to the stairs. Dad was making lunch, and Mum, Aunt Laura and Uncle Pete were going for a walk in the snow. No one was around to see where she was going. Amelia hurried up the stairs, trying not to let them creak. Hopefully Dad would think she was playing outside, too.

She tiptoed along the passageway and opened the little wooden door. Shining the torch beam ahead of her, she crept up the stairway to the attic. The coat was still there, draped over the armchair, and she could see the diary sticking out of the pocket. She'd left the blanket there, too, and Amelia wrapped it round her before she settled herself in the chair and drew out the diary, opening it eagerly to the first page.

She had thought about the diary all yesterday afternoon, and when she'd gone to write in her own diary last night, she'd flicked through it, thinking how different the two little books looked. Her diary had a pretty silver padlock, and a flowered cover, and a page at the front for her name and address. But that had made her think – wouldn't the boy still have written his name on the first page, even if his diary was just a worn cloth-bound notebook? And there it was – written on the inside of the cover:

Noah Allan

Wisconsin, 1873

The painter! This boy had grown up to paint that amazing campfire scene downstairs. And this had been his house.

Amelia stroked the pages gently and

began to read. The spelling was odd in places, and there were some words she just didn't know. Was a creek a river, maybe? And what was a snare? But even with the spiky, difficult writing, it felt amazing to be reading something written over a century before her own time. And the more of the diary she read, the easier it was to work out the words, and the strange phrases didn't seem so strange after a while. Noah's life in the woods sounded so interesting – so different to hers.

It was probably just that she was sleepy, Amelia thought, after waking in the middle of the night, but she could almost hear Noah's voice. As though he was talking to her. As though he was telling the story himself…

19th October, 1873

Pa called to me to put the lantern out, so I couldn't finish writing this last night.

I had some dried blackberries in my coat pocket so I spread them out on the snow for the pup, and dashed home while he was snuffling around eating them up. I told Ma I was going back out because I'd forgotten my muffler, and she was baking so she didn't really pay attention. I took an old blanket from the store chest up in my loft room, and got it out of the cabin without her seeing. Then I went to the lean-to and cut off a little bit of frozen pork. I reckoned we could spare it.

The pup danced up to me when I came back. He'd eaten all the dried berries, and there was a pattern of little paw prints in the snow where he'd trotted round looking for more. I'd known he'd eat them all, of course I had. But seeing him so eager and hungry-looking still, it made me worry about how much he needed to eat. I couldn't keep stealing food for him from the cabin. It wouldn't be fair on Ma. And besides, she'd soon notice. I'll be lucky if she doesn't see I took the pork.

The pup got a surprise when he tried to bite into it. He's never had frozen meat before, I guess. We depend on it, in the winter. Pa only kills the pig when the weather's cold enough to freeze the meat. This year he killed a bear, too, so we've got plenty of meat for the winter. But not enough to feed a wolf as well.

Unless I can find his mother and give

him back, the pup's going to have to learn to hunt for himself.

I went back to see him early this morning, and he was just where I'd left him, tucked up and snoozing in that old hollow tree I found last summer, not far off the path to the spring. I reckon it should be safe – it's always me that fetches the water. I've made him a little nest out of that old blanket, and he looked snug as anything. He let me walk right up to the tree before he awoke and growled a little.

The more I watch him, the more I can see he's too young to be by himself. All he wants to do is play and have someone bring him his food. I trapped a rabbit for him today. Had to tell Ma that a fox or something had torn up one of the snares. She said it was just bad luck I hadn't caught anything, but I hate lying to her.

Ma and Pa thought I'd gone out to do some drawing this morning, when I'd sneaked off to see the pup. I was supposed to be helping with the stable work. Tonight Pa lectured me on sticking to my chores and taking better care of Russet and Ruby and Lucy, and how we all had to depend on each other, so now I feel really guilty.

That's not what sticks in my mind, though. I just keep thinking of the pup, and the way his ears pricked forward when he saw it was me and he bounded out of that hollow tree to lick my fingers. Grace would have loved to play with him. I can't let him starve, can I?

CHAPTER
FOUR

Amelia twitched and wriggled sleepily, trying to find her pillow. It had hitched up, somehow, and now she was pressed against the wall. And she must have kicked off her duvet, too, she was so cold. Amelia gave up trying to reach for them with her eyes shut and sat up.

There was no pillow, and no duvet, either. She wasn't even in her bed. Amelia clutched the hairy brown blanket, the only thing that seemed familiar, and tried to work out where she was. Slowly, it came back to her – that she'd gone upstairs to the attic. She must have fallen asleep in that battered old armchair. But it didn't feel like she was still curled up there – the chair was comfy, even if it was falling apart. Now it felt as if she was sitting on straw.

She peered through the dimness, trying to see where she was. It had to be morning – she could see chinks of light showing round the door, over on the other side of the little room. But if she was in the attic, there would be light coming through the windows in the roof. Had she gone sleepwalking, and found her way to another room of the house?

It was then that the dark shape next to her – she'd taken it to be another piece of furniture – suddenly moved and blew a gust of hot breath down her neck.

Amelia squeaked and jumped sideways, and then scrambled up, reaching for the door. What was that? Where was she? She wrestled with the strange, bulky latch, all the time waiting to feel that hot breath again, as whatever it was came to eat her.

Something snorted, and there was a heavy shuffling, and as Amelia managed to pull open the door at last, she saw where she was.

The cold white glow of sun on snow
lit up the little stable, and the cow that
Amelia had been lying next to watched
her curiously. In the stall beyond, two
horses eyed her over the wooden partition,
ears flickering with interest.

There were no animals at Allan House.
Except for Freddie, of course. And Tom,
if she was being mean.

This was not the house she had gone to sleep in.

It wasn't even the winter she had gone to sleep in, Amelia decided, standing in the doorway and looking out at the huge drifts of snow. That couldn't have built up overnight. It looked like days or even weeks of snow – someone had dug a path between the drifts, leading to the stable, and the snow stood in great walls on either side.

Amelia frowned. Something about that seemed familiar, but she wasn't quite sure why. *Digging their way out* – it was what Noah had said, in his diary. There were drifts up to the eaves of the cabin, and he and his pa had to dig their way to the stable each morning.

It was just like the diary. Amelia shut her eyes for a moment, counted to ten and opened them again, but she hadn't woken up. And it didn't feel like a dream. She was *in* the diary.

Slowly, she let the door swing shut and sank down next to it. Her eyes were getting used to the dimness, and it helped that now she knew what all the strange shapes were. She could still just about see the two horses, and the dark bulk of the cow. She was quite a small cow, Amelia realized. Not as big as the ones they'd seen in the fields on their drive up to Scotland. But even a small cow was a lot bigger than Freddie, which was odd, because Amelia didn't feel very scared of her. And that didn't make sense.

Amelia gave a little snort of laughter, and one of the horses whinnied in surprise.

"Sorry…" she murmured. "Nothing about this makes sense, that's all.

69

That's why I laughed. I can't be here! Maybe I'm not," she added thoughtfully. "Maybe I'm still dreaming." Carefully, she picked her way across the hay-strewn floor and went to stroke the velvet noses of the horses.

"You feel ever so real to me. And this stable *smells* real. Not to be rude," she added hastily, "but I don't usually dream smells, and I think your stable needs cleaning. I suppose you must be Russet and Ruby. He said you were beautiful and you are. And you must be Lucy," Amelia added. She wasn't quite sure about stroking the cow. She had been riding a couple of times at the local stable and she liked horses, but she'd never met a cow before. Did they bite?

"Noah wrote that you were sad because

your calf was sold," she murmured. "And that you stood on his foot and it swelled up, but he thought you probably didn't mean to."

The horses' ears flickered again, and Amelia stepped back as one of them stamped and snorted.

"Did I scare you?" she whispered.

But the horses weren't paying her any attention now – they were looking eagerly towards the door. Amelia turned to look, too, and heard footsteps crunching through the snow.

"Someone's coming!" she hissed. She looked wildly around the stable, trying to see if there was somewhere in the shadows she could hide. But the stable was tiny – all she could see was a tangle of harnesses hanging up in the corner. She crouched behind it hurriedly, hoping that whoever was coming wouldn't stay long.

She peered round the harnesses as the door opened and a boy who looked a couple of years older than she was dashed in, banging his mittened hands together against the cold. A tall, bearded man followed him inside, wearing a fur hat just like the one Amelia had found in the attic.

"I swear it's freezing harder than ever out there," the boy said, as he wedged the door half open with a chip of wood.

Amelia tried not to lean out too far from behind the harnesses, but she was so desperate to listen to them talking. The boy sounded American, but not like on television, she thought, frowning. Different – harder to understand. Maybe like people talked in America a hundred and fifty years ago… And they both definitely had old-fashioned clothes – great clunky leather boots and woollen coats. Amelia peered through the dimness in the stable and swallowed. The coat the boy was wearing, that was the coat with the wooden buttons from the trunk. She recognized the pattern, those big brown checks.

"Hey, Ruby, hey, Russet. Good girl, Lucy. Brought your hay, look." The boy bustled around the stable, filling the nets with fresh hay, while the man – his father, Amelia guessed – swept up the soiled straw on the floor. Amelia shrank back as far behind the harnesses as she could, pulling up some straw around her knees. The boy looked quite friendly – he had dark, floppy hair like Tom's, but his eyes were softer, blue instead of brown. He looked – nicer. Maybe it was just that whenever Amelia saw Tom he was being sneery about people who were scared of dogs. But however kind the boy was, his father seemed stern. He had a black beard, and huge black eyebrows that made him look as though he was scowling. He didn't seem to talk much either.

The boy was petting the horses, and murmuring to them as he refilled their water buckets, and the man clapped him gently on the shoulder. "I'll go back and chop the wood, Noah. Come and help me when you've finished the stable work, you hear? I'll need the chips picking up."

"Yes, Pa."

Noah watched his father stride away between the snowdrifts, and sighed. "I've got to go out and check on the pup, though. Maybe Pa won't notice how long I've been."

Amelia saw him stop petting the horses – his fingers clenched into fists and he shook his head angrily. "I've got to keep him fed. And what if he wanders off? If he goes too close to the Wrights' place, they'll shoot him. I can't let that happen.

I can't… I have to help him. I've got to keep him alive, however hard it is." Then he added, in a whisper so low that Amelia could only just hear, "It's just like last year. I couldn't save Grace. I'm not letting it happen again…"

Amelia frowned. He had mentioned Grace a few times in the diary – talking about things they'd done together, or how he missed her. Amelia had thought Grace was one of his friends, and maybe she'd moved away. But then he'd talked about Grace being in trouble for tearing her dress, and his ma having to mend it.

So she must have been his sister. Amelia's stomach twisted as she suddenly realized. Grace was Noah's sister. His little sister, and she'd died. That was why his voice had been so shaky. Now he was leaning against the nearest horse's neck to hide that he was crying.

Amelia swallowed. He'd said that Grace was pale and tired, and talked about her coughing all the time. But Amelia had never thought that meant she'd died. Probably it wasn't that unusual to lose a brother or sister, living out in the woods with no doctor anywhere near. And even if the doctor could get to you, there were no antibiotics, hardly even any painkillers back then. Amelia's teacher had told her class that it wasn't that long ago that people thought eating a fried mouse was a good cure for whooping cough.

"But how am I supposed to find enough to feed him? Especially with Pa already watching me like a hawk. I reckon the pup's been slowly starving these last few days, he's so hungry," Noah muttered.

Amelia wrapped her arms round her knees and stared at the boy quietly stroking the horse's neck. She could do it. She could go and check on the pup for Noah. Except – it was a wolf, and a wolf was an even scarier sort of dog. With bigger teeth, probably. Amelia didn't go near dogs, ever. She'd only been up in the attic and found the diary because she'd been trying to stay *away* from a dog!

But why else was she here? If it wasn't all just a very, very real sort of dream, she'd travelled into the time of Noah's diary, back nearly a hundred and fifty years and halfway across the world. There had to be a good reason for something like that. Amelia tried to think how she would feel if anything happened to Bella. She couldn't imagine not having her big sister around. Bella didn't fuss over Amelia, exactly, but she always looked out for her.

Amelia was pretty sure that Noah had looked out for Grace, too. He must have felt so guilty when there was nothing he could do to help her. Worrying about the wolf pup was bringing all those feelings back.

Amelia pushed the harnesses aside and stood up, a tiny, determined figure in her scarlet hoodie and furry slipper boots. There was straw stuck in her curly black hair, but she didn't care. She scuffed the floor with her feet, so that the boy heard her and turned round sharply.

Noah gaped at her.

Amelia stared back and tried to smile. "Hello," she murmured.

"What are you doing?" he said at last. "Where did you come from?" He took a step towards Amelia and reached out, his hand wavering. But he didn't quite dare to touch her. He drew his hand back, as though he thought she might not be there and that his hand might go right through.

Seeing him almost more scared than she was made Amelia feel braver. She managed more of a smile. "I'm not a ghost, if that's what you're thinking." Then she stopped. "I don't think so, anyway. I'm definitely alive, but I might be a dream... Or you are – I'm not sure."

He snorted and folded his arms. "I'm not a dream. How did you get here?"

"I just woke up here." Amelia shoved her hands into her hoodie pockets, wondering how much to tell him. "I read your diary," she said slowly. "I don't really understand how this is happening, but I think I'm supposed to help you with the wolf pup. The one you've got hidden in the hollow tree out by the spring."

Noah glared at her angrily. "You were listening. Eavesdropping. And you can't have read my diary. It's in my coat pocket."

He went pink then, as though he realized he shouldn't have said that.

"I have. You know I have, if you think about it," Amelia pointed out. "I was listening just now – I couldn't help it, you were right next to me. But you didn't say anything about where the wolf was, did you? You think the pup belongs to the wolf that Joshua Wright shot a couple of days ago." She grinned. "And you think Joshua Wright's a skinny beanpole with ears like jug handles. You said so."

There was silence for a moment, while the two of them gazed at each other.

"You did read it…" Noah whispered. "I wrote that." He stepped closer to her, looking her up and down. He raised one hand and didn't quite touch her dark curls. "When I first saw you in the corner, I thought you were…" He gulped. "I thought you were Grace. My sister. You know what happened to her, don't you? If you've read the diary."

Amelia nodded. "I think so. I'm so sorry. I haven't read all of it but I know she died…" Her voice went very small. "I'm sorry." She didn't know what to say to him.

"She had a cough, and it wouldn't go," he said slowly. "It got worse, so she could hardly breathe. She couldn't eat, and she just slept all the time, and she only woke up when she coughed. And then she just didn't wake up any more. You look like her, a bit. Same size. Same curly hair. But I think you're older – you sound older."

"Everyone says I'm small," she admitted. "I'm nine. My name's Amelia."

"Gracie was only six. She'd be seven, now."

Amelia nodded again. She couldn't think of anything else to say.

"What are you wearing?" he demanded suddenly, and Amelia almost laughed, she was so surprised.

"A hoodie. Does it look strange? I suppose you don't have them."

"You've got trousers on!" He sounded quite shocked, and Amelia fought not to giggle. "I know. I suppose girls don't ever wear trousers here."

"Well, if you're staying, you can't wear those things." He swallowed, and added gruffly, "Suppose I could find you one of Grace's dresses, if you like. And her cap and shawl. You'll need them, if you're coming out in the snow to see the pup."

"You'd really let me wear her things?"
Amelia whispered.

He shrugged. "You look like her," he
said again. "And you've come to help. You
said so. You know all those things about
me, things you shouldn't be able to know.
So someone sent you, they must have done.
I wanted help, and I guess you're it."

Amelia nodded. He didn't look all that
impressed – and considering how she
was with dogs, he was probably right not
to be. But like he said, something had
brought her here. Some sort of magic
from the diary, maybe, or a link passed
down through their family.

I suppose Grace was my ancestor, too,
Amelia thought sadly. *Perhaps I can help
him for her.*

20th October, 1873

Just writing this quickly while I look in the old trunk for some of Gracie's clothes. I shouldn't be, because someone's waiting for me, but I need to think.

There's a girl in the stable. I don't know how she got there, or where she's come from, but she's read my diary. This diary. How can that be? I've never shown it to anyone. But she knew things about me, and about Grace, and the wolf pup.

The girl – Amelia – says that she doesn't know how it's happened, either, but she says she can help with the wolf pup – and I need the help. Should I trust her? I want to, but I think that's because she looks a little like Grace. She has curls like Grace's, and the same dark eyes, but her

face is rounder. Not so pale and tired-
looking. When I first saw her, I wanted
to rush and swing her round in the air
and make her squeal. I thought she was
Grace, hiding so she could jump out at
me, but then I remembered that won't ever
happen again.

I'm letting her borrow Grace's clothes,
because hers are all wrong. She's got
trousers on, which isn't proper for a young
lady.

It will be strange to see her in Grace's
brown print dress.

CHAPTER
FIVE

Amelia stood by the side of the cabin, shivering in her hoodie. She should have waited in the stable, where it was warmer and there was less danger of Noah's mother or father seeing her. But she couldn't just stay there, hiding in the dark. So she had followed Noah, watching him hurry through the wooden door. She'd heard him say something – to his mother, she supposed. Then Amelia had crept after him, and up to the tiny window. How could she not look? It was another world.

She stood at the side, where she couldn't be seen from indoors, and peeped carefully through. Noah had gone, upstairs she guessed, but his mother was there, in a dark green print dress and an apron, leaning over a fat, black iron stove.

Was she setting bread to rise, perhaps? Amelia wasn't sure, but the covered pans she was carrying looked as though they could be bread. Amelia frowned. Her mother made bread sometimes, and Amelia helped. But not every day!

From what she'd read in the diary, the nearest town was a day's journey away, which meant that Noah's mother had to make everything. All the food – and probably most of the family's clothes, too. Now she thought about it, Noah had written that the new shirts his mother had sewn for him weren't as soft and worn as the old ones. Amelia had a feeling that Noah's mother didn't have a sewing machine, not even an old hand-turned one. She would have to take very good care of Grace's dress, she thought, wondering how long it had taken to stitch together.

Noah's mother turned away from the stove and Amelia whisked sideways, hoping she hadn't seen a shadow at the window. She stood pressed against the wooden wall, shivering. Seeing the cabin – such a small space for three people, four until a few months ago – had made her understand that she was actually here.

This was *real*, it wasn't just a dream, or one of those school trips where the class dressed up and tried to live like people in the past. She was here, in someone's real life, for a reason.

"How big is the pup?" Amelia asked, as she followed Noah through the snow. He looked back at her curiously, and she shrugged. "I don't know very much about wolves. I've never seen one for real, I've only seen pictures of them."

Amelia swallowed, tugging Grace's shawl tighter round her shoulders, and trying not to look as though she was scared. Noah was suspicious enough already. She didn't want to admit that she was terrified at the thought of meeting a wolf – even a little one. If she could convince Noah that she wasn't scared, maybe she could convince herself. After all, why had she ended up here, if it wasn't to help Noah and the pup? There had to be a reason this was all happening – she couldn't spoil it by being frightened.

"I guess he'd come up to just below your waist," Noah said, looking at her thoughtfully. "I reckon he's about three or four months old. He must have been born late in the year. Really late. Usually wolves have their pups in the springtime, so that by the time it's cold like this, they're big enough and strong enough to hunt with the rest of the pack. So either he came along late, or he's the runt of the litter, maybe."

"The rest of the pack…" Amelia's voice wavered. "Yes. Wolves hunt in packs, don't they? So … why's this wolf all on his own? Are you sure the others aren't here, too?" She glanced sideways, almost expecting to see dark shapes slinking after them through the trees.

"There is a wolf pack," Noah explained. "When my pa first built our cabin, a few years back, he'd see them every so often, and close by. But they don't usually hunt around here any more. Pa says he sees their tracks beyond the river sometimes, but not in this stretch of the woods. Too many hunters like Pa about, you see. Wolves are clever and they're cautious, too." He frowned. "Which is why I don't really understand the mother wolf sniffing around the Wrights' place."

Amelia nodded. "Me neither. Why was she all on her own?"

Noah shrugged. "Wolves go off like that sometimes, if they want to start a new pack. But I don't think that's what this is. It's more of an accident, I reckon. She's got this tiny pup. Maybe the others had to move on to find a fresh hunting ground, and he was too little to go with them, so they both had to stay behind. If she's been trying to care for the pup, without the rest of the pack to hunt for her, she's getting desperate. When Joshua shot at her, the pup must have been frightened off. She couldn't follow him, I suppose, if she was hurt. So she holed up somewhere till she was better." He frowned. "By the river, maybe. There's a load of caves up there, and it's close to where Samson Wright said they were when Joshua shot her. Then by the time she was well enough to look for him, she'd lost the pup's trail, with the snow falling."

Amelia was silent for a moment, as they trudged on through the snow. The trees were heavy with it, and the whole forest was eerily quiet. "Would they ever be able to go back to the pack?" she asked. "Are they outcasts forever?"

Noah looked round, frowning. "I just don't know. I hope not. I was thinking, if I feed him for a little while, get his strength up so he could travel, and if we find his mother, maybe they'd be able to go after the others." He sighed, and Amelia saw his shoulders slump. "If, if, if… He might not even be at the hollow tree any more. He could have wandered off again. And how are we going to find his mother? Every time it snows, any tracks she leaves get covered up, too."

"It doesn't help that the last person she saw shot her, either," Amelia said. "She's not going to be friendly, is she?"

They stared at each other, until Noah

saw Amelia's eyes widen.

"What is it?"

Amelia wrapped her arms round herself, tucking her mittened hands under the shawl to stop them shaking. He was there.

The wolf pup was standing on the path, looking at them hopefully. His ears were pricked up and his eyes looked bright and curious. He scratched at the ground uncertainly with one paw, and looked from Noah to Amelia and back again.

Noah gave a little snort of laughter. The pup couldn't have asked, *Who's she?* any more clearly if he'd spoken out loud. He was used to Noah, but the girl was new, and new was dangerous.

"There he is," Noah said proudly, nudging her. "Must have heard us talking. He's a smart one. Look at him, eyeing you up."

"Yes…" Amelia whispered. The way Noah had been talking about the wolf, calling him a pup, and the runt of the litter, she had hoped that she wouldn't be scared. He was only a baby, after all.

But the wolf pup's dark eyes were fixed on her, and she could see him sniffing the air, trying to catch her scent. He didn't look helpless to Amelia, not at all. He was a hunter – much more frightening than any normal dog she'd hidden from back home. Her fingers twisted in the fringe of the shawl, and she gulped air, trying to breathe away the panicked dizziness inside her.

"Are you scared of him?" Noah sounded doubtful – actually, he almost sounded like Tom. A little burst of angry pride surged through Amelia, making her shake her curls and set her shoulders back.

"No." It wasn't true, of course, but she glared at Noah as if he'd said something stupid, and then – slowly, carefully – held out one hand towards the wolf. "Here, boy…"

20th October, 1873 – later on

So I did it. I took Amelia to meet the pup.
She was scared, but she hid it well. Even
the pup believed her, after a little while.
I could tell by the way the colour drained
out of her cheeks, and the way she set
her teeth together when she stroked the
pup. She made herself do it, though.

He's not even that big. I could see her
being scared of a big old dog wolf, but not
this little pup. Perhaps she's been bitten,
and she doesn't like dogs? I can't imagine
what that must be like. He's so friendly,
and good-natured, I don't understand how
someone could be scared of him. I do
worry about his mother, though, and what
she'll think of us if she gets well enough to
come looking for him. She won't understand

we were trying to help. To her, we'll just smell like danger. Amelia's right – the mother wolf will see us as the same people who hurt her and made her lose her pup in the first place.

It was odd to see Amelia trying to pet him, and flinching as he nuzzled up at her. She looks so like Grace, especially in my sister's dress. Grace would have loved him. Grace wouldn't have wanted to give him back, she'd probably have smuggled him into the house and tried to feed him cheese.

The pup seemed to understand that the girl was nervous. He didn't jump about all over her, like he does with me. I led them both back over to the hollow tree, and we gave him the food I'd brought. I showed Amelia his little nest of blankets and how cosy it was, but she shivered.

"He's out here all on his own..." she said. "Do you think he's frightened?"

I told her probably. He's only young, after all.

She looked at me when I said that, and nodded. The pup had finished his food and he came back to us, wagging his tail and looking happy. He was dancing about, nearly tripping over his own fat paws. He made her laugh, and she reached out to stroke his ears – and this time she almost looked like she enjoyed it.

Then she said, "What's his name?"

I looked at her with my mouth open. I hadn't even thought about it. I suppose because I know we can't keep him, I just think of him as the pup. But I think if he has a name, it will be easier for her to help look after him. She might not find him as frightening if she can call him something.

Amelia knows how to get to the spring now, so she can bring him his food. That means if I get some time away from the cabin, I can go looking for his mother. Then we can bring him back.

She named him Frost.

CHAPTER
SIX

Amelia sat on a fallen tree and watched Frost sniffing about in the fresh snow. He had eaten the scraps that Noah had given her and then he'd looked at her hopefully, nosing at Amelia's pockets as though he thought she might have something else hidden away.

"Noah's right," Amelia murmured, as she watched Frost look suspiciously at his own tail, and then start to whirl round and round, chasing it with fierce little growls. "You do eat a lot. Noah said he'd go and check his snares later." She shuddered at the thought of the poor rabbits, but Noah's family lived by hunting. She knew they only caught what they needed to survive, but she still didn't like it. At least Noah hadn't asked her to go and check the snares for him.

"And now he's got to feed me as well as you. I think between us we got most of his breakfast." She sighed. "I wish I could do something to help." She sank her chin into her hands and stared down at her snow-soaked boots. She still wasn't sure why she had come here. It must have been for a reason – to help, somehow. But Amelia wasn't feeling very useful.

Frost stopped dancing after his tail and padded over to her. He rested his heavy muzzle on her lap, and Amelia swallowed hard. Even yesterday, she would have been terrified. His mouth was open a little, and she could see his teeth. Frost was far from fully grown, but his jaws were strong. Deep down inside, she was still scared of him. But he was so warm against her knees, and his eyes sparkled with mischief. He seemed to know that Amelia was sad, and he waggled his whiskers at her. She giggled and gently cupped her mittened hands on either side of his head. "You're funny. Funny little wolf." There were flakes of snow caught in the grey-white fur round his muzzle, and they glittered in the faint sunlight – he looked like he had been dusted with sugar. Amelia brushed them away gently, and Frost slumped on to her feet with a contented little *oooof*.

"That's nice," Amelia murmured. "My feet are damp. I wish I'd come time-travelling in snow boots, not slippers. Grace's boots are good, but they don't keep the snow all the way out." She shivered. It was growing colder – the light was fading. She'd have to set off back to the stable soon. Noah had piled up more straw for her to hide behind, even though he'd promised Amelia that it was almost always him doing the stable chores. Then he'd looked sideways at her. "You can't just disappear, then, if my pa turns up?"

Amelia had shaken her head. "I'm not a … a fairy, or something. I don't even know how I got here. I definitely don't know how to go back again."

She had slept last night curled up on the straw, wrapped in layers of blankets. Noah had explained that the stable was one of the warmest places to be –

probably warmer than his loft bedroom. Ruby, Russet and Lucy warmed the air, and Amelia would be cosy. She hadn't quite believed him, she was sure she'd be frozen, but it was true. She hadn't been cold at all. She hadn't even woken until he'd come to feed the animals in the morning.

Frost was lying across her feet now, with his nose settled on his paws, and Amelia eyed him regretfully. He looked so comfy, and he really was helping her feet. She could almost feel her toes again, for the first time in an hour or so.

"I have to go," she whispered, but Frost only grunted and didn't move, even when something rustled among the trees across the clearing. Amelia was sure she saw a rabbit peep out at them, but Frost didn't look bothered. He was sleepy after his meal, and his game.

"Oh, well... Maybe just a few more minutes. It's getting darker, though. I suppose it does get dark early here, in the winter." Amelia squinted up at the scrap of sky she could see through the trees. It was yellowish, now the sun had disappeared, and there were heavy clouds gathering.

Frost looked up, and sniffed curiously at a fat white snowflake circling down towards his nose. His jaws snapped together sharply, and he looked up at Amelia in surprise as he felt the cold on his tongue.

"Snowing again..." Amelia stood up, looking around worriedly. It seemed even darker than it had done seconds before, and there was another snowflake, and another and another. And now they weren't just floating down out of those yellowish clouds, they were whirling and gusting all around her.

She would never be able to find her way back to the cabin in this blizzard. Amelia glanced down at Frost, who had laid his ears back, and looked just as worried as she did by the sudden storm. She didn't want to leave him out here on his own, either.

The pup let out a tiny whimper, and pressed himself against Amelia's legs. Even though she was frightened by the storm, Amelia felt herself smiling. He trusted her. He was scared and he trusted her to help! She stared determinedly around at the clearing, squinting through the snowflakes as she tried to work out what to do. "I'm not going back to the stable," she murmured, rubbing Frost's ears gently. "I'm not leaving you behind. So it's the hollow tree or nothing. Come on. It'll be a bit of a squash, but at least we'll keep each other warm…"

She hurried him over to the tree and crouched down, trying not to think about what else might be sharing the hollow with them. It was too cold for spiders, she told herself firmly, as Frost wriggled in after her. Then he turned to peer out of the opening and whimpered.

"I know," Amelia whispered to him. "It's horrible, isn't it?" She loved snow, but she had never seen it like this. The snowflakes were falling so thickly that she could hardly see across the little clearing.

Frost stepped away from the jagged opening in the tree and whimpered again, curling himself against the back of the trunk. The wind had shifted, and now the snow was starting to blow into the hole, stinging his eyes.

Amelia sucked in an anxious breath. The hollow tree was a wonderful shelter, even though it was cramped with the two of them in there. But it would be no good at all if it filled up with snow. She looked doubtfully at the thick woollen blanket that Noah had given Frost to sleep on. She wasn't sure if it was much use against snow, but it was all they had. Wriggling it half out from under herself and Frost, she held it up against the opening, tucking the edge into a useful crack that went higher up the tree trunk. She wedged it with a couple of slivers of bark, too, so that the blanket hung down across the hole, shielding them from the worst of the snow. Then she edged back next to Frost and ran her hand gently over his twitchy ears.

"You don't like it, do you? Maybe you've never seen a big snowstorm. Or if you have, you were huddled up in a nice cosy cave with your mum and you didn't mind."

Amelia unwound the green and red checked muffler that Noah had given her. He'd had to show her how to wind it crosswise over her chest and tie it at the back – Amelia had never worn anything like it before. She laid it out on her lap, and patted it hopefully. With the blanket hung up as a curtain, Frost was sitting on a cushion of dried leaves and pine needles. She was sure that snuggling up with the muffler wrapped round them would be more comfortable. And they needed to keep each other warm.

Frost lifted his nose from his paws and looked up at her worriedly. She could see

his eyes shining in the shadowy dimness
of the hollow tree. The whirling madness
of the snowstorm had clearly upset him.
But at last he wriggled forward a little
bit, and very gradually, he climbed
half into Amelia's lap. There was too
much of him to curl up like a cat, but
he slumped across her knees, and sighed
contentedly.

"We'll just have to stay here till it stops," Amelia whispered. "I wish I hadn't given you all the food, but I didn't know this was going to happen…" She wrapped her arms round Frost's neck, and he made a happy grumbling noise. "The snow's too heavy for Noah to come and find us," she murmured into his fur. "I hope he doesn't try. We'll be all right till morning. He'll come and find us then." She was trying to sound determined and hopeful, but her voice wavered a bit, and Frost nosed gently at her cheek.

It was eerie, in the dark. She could see the odd flake of snow settling on the edge of the blanket here and there, but that was all. The snow was silent, but that only seemed to make it more frightening. Amelia sat in their hollow, peering out at

the little smudge of snowy darkness, and
stroking Frost's silvery fur over and over
again.

21st October, 1873

She's not back. The snowstorm came down
so suddenly while Amelia was still out in
the woods with Frost. I tried to go and
fetch her, but I had to stop before I
got halfway. I couldn't see. My eyelashes
had ice on them, and it was all round my
nose and mouth, too, even with a muffler
wrapped round.

I got back to the cabin and Pa was
furious - he grabbed me and hugged me
first, and then he took me by the shoulders
and shook me and told me to promise him
I'd never go out in a storm like that
again.

I guess I nodded, and he let me be. I
couldn't say it out loud, but I want to be

out there now, finding them! Instead I'm sat inside in the warmth of the stove, full of Ma's stew and pancakes. But I've got a stash of pancakes wrapped in a cloth in my coat pocket.

As soon as it's light, I'll go. Whatever Pa thinks, I don't care. If he won't let me, I'll tell him and Ma about Amelia, and Frost. I don't care who finds them, as long as someone does.

CHAPTER
SEVEN

"Amelia! Amelia! Are you there?"

Amelia felt Frost wriggle on her lap and she sat up, groaning. She was stiff all over and so cold that she could hardly feel her fingers. But they were safe! They had slept through the snowstorm together, and there was sparkling snow-white light glowing round the edges of the blanket now.

"Amelia! Frost!"

"Oh, Noah!" Amelia leaned forward, and tried to pull back the blanket. Perhaps he couldn't see where they were.

It was stuck, and she had to shift the sleepy, grumpy wolf mostly off her knees to yank at it. And then the blanket came away, all at once, and quite a lot of snow came with it, crumpling down on top of the grey wool. Even so, there was an awful lot of snow left. A wall of it, built up in front of the hole in the tree, white and rippled and slightly glittery. Amelia gaped at it. The hole in the tree was at least a metre tall, and it was almost all covered up. There was just a patch of light coming in at the top. Had all that snow fallen in one night?

Frost whined anxiously, and clawed at the snowdrift with a cautious paw.

"I think we're going to have to dig our way out," Amelia agreed, pushing at the wall of snow with her mitten.

"Amelia! Is that you?" called Noah.

Amelia giggled suddenly. "How many other friends have you got buried in snowdrifts out in these woods?"

There was a scuffling, and the patch of light got larger as two grey-gloved hands dug into it. "Very funny. I was worried about you! Real worried. I tried to come and find you last night, but Pa wouldn't let me leave the house in the snowstorm. I imagined you freezing to death out here. And then… Well, I wondered if you'd gone back to wherever it was you came from."

Amelia smiled up at him. "Hopefully that won't happen until we've taken Frost back to his mother. And you didn't need to worry about us, we kept each other warm. Warmish, anyway." She rubbed Frost's soft head thoughtfully. "It would have been worse for him if he was all on his own. The snow would have blown in and swamped him."

"You did well to pin the blanket up," Noah told her gruffly, as he worked away at the wall of snow. Frost and Amelia helped from the inside, scrabbling and digging, until at last Frost could scramble out into the clearing again. Noah then hauled Amelia out and they watched the little wolf race around, sinking chest-deep into the soft new snow and yelping like a mad thing.

"I don't think he liked being shut up," Amelia said, laughing.

Noah grimaced. "It's good he's got some life in him. He's going to need to make a trip. The Wrights came by our cabin early this morning, to warn us. I'd have been here before if I hadn't stayed to listen to what they were saying. They heard a wolf around their house last night."

"Frost's mother!" Amelia gasped.

"I think so." Noah nodded. "There can't be two lone wolves hunting around here all of a sudden, can there? Samson Wright says he thinks he knows where she's hiding out. There are some caves along the bank of the river, like I told you yesterday. Mr Wright reckons she's there, too. He came by to see if we'd heard her. He said he was going back home to…"

He swallowed. "To melt down some lead and make more bullets for their guns. And then he and Joshua are setting off to follow her tracks – they say it shouldn't be too hard, with the fresh snow. I think they wanted Pa to go with them, but you know he's not sure there even is a wolf." Noah glanced sideways at Amelia. "They're going to shoot her."

"No!" Amelia whispered. "We can't let them." She crouched down as Frost came skittering up to her, tail whisking delightedly, and brushed the snow crystals from his muzzle. "I don't care if it's dangerous, Noah. Surely if we take Frost back to her, she'll know that we aren't mean like the Wrights? She'll be too pleased to see her pup even to notice us."

"Let's hope so," Noah said grimly.

"But we have to get going now, Amelia. Look, you eat these." He handed her some pancakes, wrapped in a cloth. "And I've brought some scraps for Frost, just to give him the energy for a long walk. As soon as he's eaten, we've got to go. The Wrights could have set off already. They mustn't find his mother first."

He pulled out a little tin pan, full of breakfast scraps, and set it down in front of Frost, who started to gobble them up eagerly. Amelia leaned against the tree and watched the pup, frowning worriedly. He was still so young. Would he be able to manage the long walk to the river? Would she?

"I have to," she whispered. "We have to get you both away safely. I'm not leaving you, or your mother, to the hunters."

22nd October, 1873

Amelia is feeding Frost and eating the pancakes I brought. I said I was going off to check the snares - maybe we can use the rabbits I've got to tempt his mother out? I don't know. I don't know how this is going to work at all. I can only hope and pray that it will, somehow. It makes me feel better to write this down. And to draw one last quick sketch of Frost and Amelia, while he eats up the last of the dried berries I brought for him. They can't see me, here behind this tree.

The drawing isn't very good, but it may be the last I have of them after today. If all goes well, Frost will be off across the river with his mother, to find the rest of their pack. And if it doesn't go well –

I don't want to think about that.

Whatever happens, once Frost is gone,
Amelia will go, too. I'm almost sure.

I wish... I wish they could stay.

CHAPTER
EIGHT

"How far is it to the river?" Amelia asked, as Noah kneeled in the snow, fastening on the snowshoes he had brought for her. "I don't know if I can walk in these things."

Frost sniffed curiously at the strange contraptions strapped to Amelia's boots, and she sighed and wriggled her feet. The snowshoes looked like a cross between a basket and a tennis racket, and they felt huge and heavy on the ends of her legs.

"The snow's too new and soft to walk on without them," Noah explained. "They spread your weight out. They're odd to walk in at first, but you'll get used to it. You have to take big steps, that's all. If you come after me, the snow will be squashed down a bit, anyway, so that'll make it easier."

Amelia looked at him doubtfully and then at her feet. But she didn't have a choice. The snow was so deep if she tried to walk in it without snowshoes, she would sink up to her knees. She put her hand on Noah's sleeve. "How far is it?" she asked again.

Noah fiddled with the straps a little longer and then he sighed. "A few miles. It's not really that far…"

Amelia nodded. "It'll be all right," she said. "We'll get there. We'll be in time."

She had her fingers crossed inside her mittens, hoping that it was true.

"We should stay quiet," Noah murmured, taking her arm. "The Wrights will be on their way over to the river, too. We don't want them hearing us."

Before long, Amelia had no breath to talk anyway. The snowshoes felt like lumps of lead, and the muscles in her legs were aching. But she kept on going, plodding after Noah, determined that they would reach the river.

Frost had started off the walk bright-eyed and bouncy, but after an hour of ploughing through the snow his tail was drooping, and his ears were laid flat against his head. When the path started to slope, and the drifts got deeper, he let out a miserable whimper and stopped.

Amelia balanced herself carefully on her snowshoes, and made a slow, wobbly turn. "What's up, Frost?" she whispered, gently stroking his ears. There were ice crystals on the fur round his muzzle, where his breath had frozen. He looked worn out.

"I don't think he can go much further," Noah said anxiously, crouching down to look at the little wolf. "He had a couple of days with no food at all before I found him, I reckon. It made him weak."

Amelia bent down to put her arm round Frost's thin shoulders, and he leaned against her gratefully. "I know how you feel," she muttered. "My legs hurt, too."

She looked up at Noah. "Do you think we could carry him?"

But Noah wasn't listening. "Hush a minute," he breathed. He was standing like a hunter, Amelia thought, half crouched, ready, his head slowly turning from side to side. She waited, her heart suddenly thudding against her ribs. What was it? Had the mother wolf been tracking them? Or maybe Noah's father had come out looking for him? She didn't dare move, she just crouched there, scanning the snowy whiteness. Even the darkness of the trees was half hidden now, with a fresh layer of snow over the branches.

"What is it?" she whispered at last, when she couldn't bear it any longer.

"Can't you hear?" Noah mouthed back, pointing. "Voices."

Amelia pushed back her fur-lined cap a little, and tried to listen. He was right! She could just about hear them, filtering through the trees, a word here and there.

"...Broken?"

"Stupid..."

"Who is it?" she whispered.

"The Wrights." Noah nodded fiercely. "I'm sure. I recognize that whining tone in Joshua's voice. Besides, who else would be out here?" He looked around.

"I can't see them. But they sound angry, don't you think? Maybe something's wrong. Come on…"

He led the way through the trees, shuffling quietly over the snow, until they were close enough to hear Samson and Joshua arguing. They could just see Joshua sitting in the snow, with his father leaning over him. Amelia shivered, as she saw the dark gleam of Samson's gun under his arm.

"It *is* broken!" the boy wailed, and Amelia heard Samson snort in disgust.

"No such thing. Your ankle's just twisted. How could you be so clumsy, Joshua? Come on, up with you! We need to get after that wolf. It could take us a while to track it down, and I don't want to be caught out here in the dark."

Joshua whimpered. "I can't!"

Amelia heard Samson sigh loudly, and then he grabbed a half-broken branch, and yanked it away from the tree. He cursed and dodged as several armfuls of soft snow slithered down, just missing him. "Nearly went down my neck," he muttered, shaking his coat. "Here, have this to lean on." He flung the branch at Joshua's feet.

Noah backed away slowly, leading Amelia through the dense trees until there was room to turn round in their bulky snowshoes. "We have to keep going!" he told her, as soon as they reached the path. "I know Joshua, he'll whinge and whine, but he's probably just making a fuss. And Mr Wright wants that wolf. He said so this morning. He wants a wolfskin to trade – they won't rest for long. We need to get there before they do."

Amelia nodded, and rubbed her aching knees. She could keep going. But what about Frost? The little wolf still looked exhausted – the short rest they'd had wasn't enough.

"I kept this back," Noah murmured, pulling a piece of dried meat out of his coat pocket. "Yes, you can smell it, can't you? A little bit now— Hey, not all at once, cheeky!" He chuckled quietly as Frost tried to snatch the whole piece. "It's in my pocket, pup… Yes, you follow along."

Amelia smiled as Noah set off again, this time with Frost's nose practically in his coat pocket. Obviously the meat had been so good, Frost didn't want to risk losing the rest of it. Noah was so natural with him, Amelia thought. He knew just how to tempt the pup along.

But it was me that helped keep him warm and safe last night, Amelia thought. *Without me, he might never have woken up.*

They trudged on, with Noah stopping to tear off tiny pieces of dried meat every so often, and Frost dragging himself wearily through the snow. But after another hour of hard walking, the wolf pup stopped, the snow halfway up his legs. He stood staring into the distance with his ears pricked.

"Come on, boy." Noah patted his pocket where the last scrap of meat was waiting and glanced back anxiously to see if the Wrights were coming after them.

"No, I don't think he's tired," Amelia said, seeing the eagerness in Frost's twitching nose, the way the ruff of fur round his neck was rising. "He can smell something. Look at him, Noah! Are we close? Could it be his mother?"

Noah lifted his hand to shade his eyes. The clouds had cleared and bright sun was glinting on the snow. "Yes. See there,

Amelia? Up ahead, the trees are thinning out. We're close to the river. We'd be able to hear it, if it wasn't frozen over. He must have picked up her scent."

Amelia watched as Frost danced excitedly ahead. "We're going to find her!" she said, then hurried after him, floundering in the snow.

Noah followed them, frowning worriedly. "Amelia, stay back," he murmured. "We have to be careful. She's not going to trust us."

But Amelia was too excited to listen. She was plunging after Frost, caught up in the wolf pup's joy. He was skittering here and there, sniffing and giving little whines of recognition. Then, just as Noah was reaching out to pull Amelia back, they broke through the trees to the riverbank.

Frost stopped dead, staring across the great stretch of snow-covered ice below them.

On the opposite bank, a wolf had heard them coming. She was standing guard, tall and watchful on her rock, twenty metres away across the ice.

Amelia swallowed hard. She had been so scared of Frost when she first saw him, but she loved him now. Somehow, she had assumed his mother would be just like him – only a little bigger.

But the silvery wolf poised on the stone outcrop was lean and powerful – and terrifying. As she dropped down, bounding from rock to rock, Amelia could see the strength in every leap and spring. Even Frost seemed daunted by her for a moment, as she prowled out on to the ice. But then he squeaked, and half ran, half tumbled down between the boulders to meet his mother.

Amelia and Noah watched as the pair sniffed lovingly at each other, and then Frost bounced skittishly around his mother, darting up to nudge her with his nose and nibble at her tail.

All the while, though, the mother wolf kept one eye on Amelia and Noah, and at last she stalked forward, with Frost skidding in the snow and ice as he hurried to catch up.

The wolf stopped at the edge of the river, gazing at them. Now that she was closer, Amelia could see that one of her forelegs was injured, a trail of dark dried blood was matted in the fur. What if the wolf jumped at them? To her, they must just smell of people – the people who had wounded her. Should they run away?

But although the wolf stood stiffly, her shoulders tense and ready to spring, all she did was look. Her eyes were dark and wary. Amelia wished they could tell her what had happened – that truly, all they had wanted was to save Frost and bring him home.

The wolf took one more step forward, hesitating in the narrow path between the rocks, and Amelia stretched out her hand, ignoring Noah's gasp of warning.

The girl and the wolf stared at each other, and then the silver wolf gently licked Amelia's hand, just one quick affectionate dash of her tongue – as though Amelia were another pup. And then she was gone, darting back on to the ice.

Her ears were pricked up, and she seemed to be watching the trees as she hurried Frost before her.

"It's the Wrights," Noah said, turning to look where she looked. "She can hear them, I bet. Go! Go!" He pointed across the river, and the mother wolf seemed to understand him. She loped across the ice, pushing Frost with her nose when he stopped to glance back at Noah and Amelia.

"Goodbye!" Amelia called softly, as the two wolves vanished among the rocks on the far bank of the river.

Amelia watched for a moment and then turned to Noah, her voice strangely flat as she said, "They've gone."

"Mmm." Noah swallowed, and they stared helplessly at each other. Then he looked anxiously along the riverbank again, where Frost's mother had been staring.

"Amelia, we have to cover their tracks! Frost and his mother are together again, but that doesn't mean anything if Samson and Joshua can just follow their paw prints. They'll catch them both!" He sat down on a snow-covered boulder, and started hurriedly undoing the bindings on his snowshoes.

"What do we do?" Amelia looked down at the snow where the mother wolf had been standing – the prints were so clear.

They would lead the hunters straight to Frost and his mother.

"We need to brush them away," Noah told her, jumping up and swinging on a fat fir branch. "Help me break this off. We'll use it like a yard brush, and sweep the snow. We'll start on the river. Come away, you stupid branch. Ah!"

He shook the snow out of his face, but the branch had torn off at last. "I'll get another, Amelia; you go across to the far bank and brush away their tracks. Work backwards, you see? The wind's getting up, and the snow's blowing out there in the open. If we're lucky, Samson Wright will just think the brushed bits are blown snow. I'm going to go back in among the trees a bit, and get rid of the prints we made coming."

Amelia nodded and fought with the binding to undo her own snowshoes. She edged down to the ice, and stepped on to it gingerly. How solid was it? It had taken the weight of the wolves, but she hated the thought of it creaking and cracking beneath her. But it didn't shift at all – it was like walking on a cold marble floor, and she took a deep breath of relief. Then she scrambled out on to the ice, following the delicate lines of tracks in and out of the piles of snow.

The ice was slippery under the drifts, and although she fell a couple of times, she scrambled quickly to her feet. She brushed furiously at the snow, whisking away the paw prints, and her own footprints, just as Noah had told her. The wind helped, swirling up little eddies of snow here

and there. It blew in her face, but she
didn't care. The snow disguised the trail
of her fir branch. As she worked back over
the ice, the sky darkened again, and a few
new flakes began to fall. Amelia watched
gratefully as they softly blurred the signs
of her sweeping.

She was almost back to the bank when she saw Noah, half tiptoeing through the trees, dragging the branch behind him to clear his trail.

"They're coming!" he hissed. "I saw them. Joshua's still limping. It's lucky for us he fell, Amelia. We'd never have been in time otherwise."

"Shall we hide?" Amelia asked, picking up her snowshoes. She could hear the Wrights now, too. It sounded as though Samson was telling his son to hurry up.

"Yes. Look, duck in here." Noah pushed her gently in between two large rocks, and Amelia gasped. It was a tiny cave, sheltered from the snow.

They huddled inside, listening to the stamping footsteps of the hunters, and Joshua's complaints.

Amelia wrinkled her nose. "Shouldn't they be quiet, if they're hunting?"

Noah nodded. "But it's a good sign. If they'd seen tracks, they'd be more watchful."

"Pa, it's starting to snow!"

Amelia huddled closer to Noah as a thin man tramped through the trees above them, followed by a whining boy, leaning on a branch.

"And we've not found any tracks – that wolf's long gone! I'm frozen to the bone, and my ankle hurts. Let's go home, Pa!"

Samson Wright stood staring out across the river, scowling. Amelia held her breath. Had they cleared Frost and his mother's tracks well enough?

The hunter peered down at the snow-covered river, and Amelia pressed the back of her hand against her mouth. She wanted to scream at them to go away and leave the wolves alone. She could feel the words bubbling up inside her…

"No tracks…" Mr Wright murmured.

"We've lost her," Joshua moaned. "If she was ever out this way in the first place. We've not seen a print for miles."

"I just want to go down there and take a closer look," his father murmured.

Amelia turned anguished eyes on Noah. If Mr Wright went down to the river, he'd see they'd swept the snow! She couldn't let him get any closer. If they saw the tracks, they would never give up on Frost and his mother. Samson Wright still wanted that wolfskin.

Pressing her finger to her lips, Amelia looked meaningfully at Noah, and then stood up, picking her way between the tall rocks. She was smaller than Noah was, and there was less chance that she'd be seen. Even though she was terrified of Samson Wright and his gun, she had to send them away.

Joshua was still complaining and pulling at his father's sleeve. "I can't get down there, Pa! I can't walk! It's all rocks!"

"Stay here, then!" Samson Wright snapped.

Amelia crept silently between the rocks, keeping as much cover as she could between herself and the hunters. But she couldn't take too long. She scrambled up the bank, and threaded her way between the trees, until she was just behind Mr Wright and Joshua. Then she picked up a handful of snow, and squashed it quickly into a ball. She aimed at the branches above their heads, heavy with soft, glittering snow, and hurled her snowball.

The snow shook a little, and then collapsed with a *whumpf*, right on to Samson Wright's hat, and all down the back of his coat.

He gasped, and shook
himself like a dog, and
in all the confusion
and shouting,
Amelia slipped back
down the bank to
join Noah.

"Not again! I've
had just about enough
of this. Have it your
way…" Samson Wright growled, digging
snow out of the back of his collar and
shivering. "We'll go. I was sure the beast
was out here at the river, but I've not seen
hide nor hair of it. All right, all right!
We'll go on home."

Amelia clutched Noah's arm, and
looked at him with shining eyes. The
wolves were safe!

22nd October, 1873 - later on

Amelia's fallen asleep, worn out by the journey to the river, and the excitement. She's got her head on my shoulder, and she looks so snug. But I suppose I'll have to wake her soon, as it's almost stopped snowing. Just a few more flakes, coming down all slow and lazy. It won't be long before we can set off back home.

I had my heart in my mouth when she got up like that, and went sneaking off. I had my hand out to grab her, and pull her back. But thank heaven I let her be. She made them give up, Mr Wright and Joshua. I can still see him, stamping around trying to get that snow out of his coat. It's making me chuckle, even now.

I can see across the river a little

way – all the tracks are gone. It wasn't a heavy snowfall, but it was enough.

The sun's starting to glimmer on those great icicles, where the spray comes off the rapids. I'd love to draw that, but I'm too sleepy to try.

I wonder where Frost and his mother are. I reckon they went off up the far bank of the river, and up into the hills – there are deep caves there, just right for a wolf pack. Frost's on his way home, too. I was glad he looked back at us before he went.

Maybe one day I'll see him again.

CHAPTER NINE

Amelia shivered and wriggled away from the damp tongue licking her cheek. "Don't, Frost, it's too cold to lick—"

But then she remembered. Frost had gone back to his mother. He was safe. Maybe they'd even met up with the rest of the pack by now.

So what was licking her face?

Amelia opened her eyes, and saw Freddie looking down at her, his great pink tongue sticking out. Amelia pressed herself back against the chair, her eyes widening, and her heart starting to race.

And then she saw that Freddie's ears were pricked up hopefully, just the way Frost's had been when he wanted her to play with him, or he was hoping that Noah had something delicious in the deep pockets of his coat.

The same coat Amelia could see now, draped over the old armchair in the attic.

She was back.

"Hello…" she whispered to Freddie, and his massive tail wagged so hard it bumped against the side of the chair. He had his front paws up on the seat next to her, and his head on one side, as though he was asking something.

"How did you get up here, hey? I suppose I didn't shut the door properly. Did you sniff me out? And what do you want? Oh! Are you not supposed to sit on chairs? Well, this is only an old scruffy one…" Amelia shifted herself sideways a bit, leaving a space for Freddie to leap up.

He snuggled delightedly into the gap, and sat there next to her, looking pleased with himself and panting. His tongue was huge, and it stuck out a little bit, giving him a foolish, friendly look. Amelia wondered why she had been so scared of him. His fur was browner than Frost's, but he had the same dark eyes and pointed, velvety ears.

"I suppose you're related to wolves," Amelia told him sleepily. "But I bet you've never hunted anything in your life.

Except maybe squirrels in the park."

Freddie whined hopefully at the mention of squirrels, and Amelia giggled. "No, I didn't mean I've spotted one, sorry."

The big dog sighed and flopped down half in her lap, just as Frost had that night in the hollow tree. Was that last night? Amelia frowned, trying to work it out. Last night – or hundreds and thousands of nights ago. She didn't know. Maybe it didn't matter.

Freddie sniffed curiously at her hands, and Amelia gently pulled the diary away. He'd probably chew it, if she let him.

"No, we're going to read it," she whispered, rubbing the soft fur round his ears. "I have to know the rest of the story."

"Open this one, Amelia," Mum said, handing her a small, square parcel, and smiling hopefully.

Amelia giggled as Freddie stuck his great nose over her arm to sniff at the parcel. He had several presents of his own, but he still insisted on checking out hers and Tom's, just in case they might taste good. He was sitting in between them, to make sure he didn't miss anything. And occasionally he'd pick his way through the litter of wrapping

174

paper to keep an eye on Bella and Lara and Anya.

"Is it chocolate?" Tom asked, eyeing the present. "Don't open the box in front of Freddie if it is. He thinks chocolate is the best thing in the world, just because it's really bad for dogs and he isn't allowed it. He nicked a Mars bar out of my hand once, and it was gone in one gulp. Mum rang the vet's and they said there wasn't really that much chocolate in a Mars, so it was OK. But since then he's got a taste for it…"

"I think it's too heavy to be chocolate," Amelia said, feeling the edges of the parcel. "It's quite hard, too."

"Open it!" Tom said. "Honestly, you're so slow! I'd have ripped the paper off ages ago!"

Amelia grinned. Now that she wasn't

scared of Freddie, it seemed that she wasn't scared of Tom's sharp tongue any more, either. And his dark, floppy hair reminded her of Noah. He was even quite funny sometimes. He'd pulled her and Freddie all the way back up the lane on the sledge the day before. He said Freddie didn't like having cold paws. Amelia had made Tom a cup of hot chocolate afterwards to say thank you.

Amelia peeled the paper off extra slowly, just to annoy him, and Tom slumped back on the sofa, and stared at the ceiling as if he couldn't stand it.

"Oh!" Amelia gasped and nearly dropped the parcel.

"What is it?" Tom sat up suddenly, not wanting to miss anything.

"It's a picture…"

"I thought it was something really exciting!" Tom muttered.

"It is…" Amelia whispered. But she couldn't tell him why.

"Do you like it?" Mum smiled at her. "I thought she looked a little bit like you. I wasn't sure if you'd want it, because of the wolf, but it's so beautiful. When I saw the framed print on the gallery website, and I knew we were coming here, to Noah

Allan's house, it just seemed perfect… We could go and see the real painting some time, if you like, Amelia."

"It does look like you, actually," Tom agreed, glancing between Amelia and the painting in her hands. "If you were wearing funny clothes. That bonnet thing is hilarious!"

Amelia ran her finger over the dress in the picture. Grace's brown print dress. And Frost, staring out at them, his ears pricked up as if he wanted Noah to come and play with them in the snow.

"Noah remembered us," she whispered.

22nd October, 1873 - later still

I fell asleep writing, and when I woke up, she was gone. They're both gone.

All I have left of them are the drawings in this book. If it wasn't for those, I might have thought it was all a dream. But I know that they were real.

I ought to be sad, but I'm not. I'm remembering. One day, I'll paint them both, just as I can see them in my head.

I do miss them. I miss Frost jumping around me when I brought him scraps. I miss him rolling in the snow, and making his coat glitter. I miss him barking at the birds teasing him in the trees. And I miss Amelia laughing.

She thought everything was funny, and she was so brave, just like Grace. I know

Amelia was scared of Frost. I never saw someone go that white, when he first came up to her. But she didn't run — she didn't even cry. I couldn't have saved him without her.

I wonder where they are now, both of them? My little snow sister, and my winter wolf?

THE
SNOW
BEAR

FROM BEST-SELLING AUTHOR
HOLLY WEBB

As the snow begins to fall
just days before Christmas,
Grandad helps Sara build an
igloo in the garden with a small
snow bear to watch over it.

And when Sara wakes in the
middle of the night, it looks
very different outside. She sets out
on an enchanted journey through
a world of ice, but will she ever
find her way home…

The garden looked like an illustration
from a fairy tale. Sara had seen snow
before, of course, but this was so deep,
and so clean and new, that everything
shimmered and sparkled in the thin, clear
sunlight.

"I hope it doesn't melt," Sara said to
herself, glancing up at the sky. But it didn't
feel like it would. The sunshine hardly had

any warmth in it, and she was cold, even wrapped up in her coat and long scarf. She stepped out on to the grass. At least, she thought it was the grass. She had to step carefully – she could have been standing on anything. Sara held out her hands to steady herself. She was glad that Grandad didn't have a pond – she might walk out into the middle of it in this.

"This is definitely the bit of grass between the roses and the wall," Sara muttered to herself, frowning and trying to remember the layout of the garden. She knew exactly what it looked like, almost as well as she knew her garden at home! But she'd never tried to walk round it blindfolded, and that was what it felt like.

The snow crunched and squeaked under her boots as she tracked across the lawn, admiring her footprints. It was about twenty centimetres deep, she thought. Not quite high enough to go over the top of her boots. But not far off.

Sara turned and looked back at her trail. The prints were really crisp, as though she'd shaped them with a knife. The snow was calling for her to build something in it. But not just a snowman. Somehow that wasn't right for the magical feel of the morning. Sara moulded a snowball thoughtfully, pressing it together between her gloved hands, and enjoying the feel of the snow under her fingers.

Then she smiled. Of course. Grandad's story last night. She was going to make a snow bear.

Once she had the idea, it came easily. The snow was a little powdery, but it held together well enough, and the shape she had in mind wasn't very complicated. Sara loved polar bears and she had lots of toy ones at home, of all sizes, and a little notebook with a polar bear photo on the cover.

The bear was sitting up, almost like a boy slouching against a wall, with his hind paws stuck out in front of him. So it was easy enough to heap up a mound of snow to be his back, stretching it out into two fat back paws. The head was harder – when she tried to build the snow out into a pointed bear face, it just fell off. In the end she rolled a sort of triangular snowball, and balanced it on the top, with little snowballs for ears. Then she shaped some of the body into front paws, hanging down at the sides.

Sara stood back, admiring her bear. He was almost finished, but there was something missing. She pursed her lips thoughtfully, and then sighed. The eyes. She needed some little stones, or something like that – but everything was buried under the snow. She glanced around, and managed to find a couple of dark, withered rose leaves, still just about visible under the snow covering the bushes. She pushed them into place on either side of the long white muzzle, but they didn't look quite right.

Someone laughed behind her, and she turned to see Grandad standing in the doorway.

"He's fantastic, Sara!"

She grinned at him. "He is nice," she agreed. "But he isn't finished, Grandad.

His face looks wrong. It's mostly the eyes. I can't find anything to make them out of."

Grandad nodded, and then rubbed his hands together. "I know. Give me just a minute." He hurried indoors, and came back, smiling, holding out a hand to her.

Sara tramped to the door, feeling the cold now that she'd stopped building. "Oh, they're perfect," she said delightedly, picking the bits of green sea glass from Grandad's hand. "I should have thought of that. Can I really borrow them? Won't they get lost in the snow?"

Grandad had a jar of sea glass on the kitchen windowsill, all shades of green, and even a couple of tiny blue pieces. He picked it up when he went walking on the beach, and now, when the sun shone through it on the windowsill, it looked like a tiny jarful of the sea inside the house.

"Of course you can. You'll just have to go hunting on the beach for some more if they disappear when your bear melts. I'm sure we'll spot them in the grass, though."

Sara ran back to the bear, taking out the leaves and pressing the green glass into the snow. She smiled at the difference they made to the long white face. He was suddenly real, a snow bear sitting in the garden.

She couldn't help glancing back at him, as she hurried in to eat breakfast. She had the strangest feeling that he was waiting for her to return.

The Snow Cat

FROM BEST-SELLING AUTHOR
HOLLY WEBB

An enchanting Christmas story,
perfect for bedtime reading

Christmas is approaching and Bel is staying
with Gran in her new home. The flat is part
of a grand old Victorian house with beautiful
gardens – perfect for exploring. If only Bel
had someone to play with…

One snowy morning, Bel spots a strange
white cat with golden eyes who leads her
under the branches of a large fir tree. There
she meets Charlotte, a girl from the past, who
tells her the cat belongs to her poorly sister,
Lucy. But then Snow disappears. Can Bel
help her new friend find Lucy's beloved cat?

HOLLY WEBB

Holly Webb started out as a children's book editor, and wrote her first series for the publisher she worked for. She has been writing ever since, with over one hundred books to her name. Holly lives in Berkshire, with her husband and three young sons. Holly's pet cats are always nosying around when she is trying to type on her laptop.

For more information
about Holly Webb visit:

www.holly-webb.com